I WANT IT!

Paul Meisel

I Like to Read®

HOLIDAY HOUSE • NEW YORK

Go.

Goal.

Here I go.

Go, go, go.

Here we come.

I can fly.

Look out.

What?

Beep.

Mine.

I want it.

WAH!

Help!

Roar.

What?

Roar.

I want it.

Mine.

Sniff.

Mine!

I WANT IT.
I WANT IT.
I WANT IT.

Okay.

Let's play!